The Ramayana, from which this story of Rama and Sita is taken, is one of the great epic poems of India. It was originally composed in Sanskrit by the poet Valmiki in about 300 BC, but has since been translated into many of the vernacular Indian languages. As a whole, *The Ramayana* is a combination of romantic and allegorical legends and stories, half-mythical and half-historical. The first and last books, considered to be later additions, present Rama as an incarnation of the Hindu god Vishnu, but elsewhere he is portrayed as the perfect man and king.

The Ramayana has remained popular in India throughout the centuries—many ancient paintings and carvings depict scenes from the stories and to this day in northern India the events of the poem are enacted in an annual pageant also known as the Ramayana.

For My Parents

First Published 1987 by Blackie and Son Ltd.

British Library Cataloguing in Publication Data available.

ISBN 0 216 92105 8

Blackie and Son Ltd
7 Leicester Place
London WC2H 7BP

First American edition published in 1988 by
Peter Bedrick Books
125 East 23rd Street
New York, NY 10010

Library of Congress Cataloging-in-Publication Data

Ram, Govinder.
     Rama and Sita: an Indian folk tale.

   (Folk tales of the world)
     Summary: Banished by his father to a dark forest, Prince Rama
proceeds to lose his wife to the demon prince Ravana until a tribe of
monkeys comes to help him.
     [1. Folklore—India]   I. Title.   II. Series: Folk tales of the world
(New York, N.Y.)
     PZ8.1.R128Ram   1988   398.2'2'0954 [E]   87-14333

ISBN 0-87226-171-9

Printed in Great Britain by Cambus Litho.

An Indian Folk Tale

Rama and Sita

Folk Tales of the World

Govinder Ram

**BEDRICK/BLACKIE
NEW YORK**

**BLACKIE
LONDON**

Once long ago in India, in the kingdom of Ayodha, there lived a king called Dasaratha. He was growing old and tired, and he decided that it was time to pass on the kingdom to his favourite son, Prince Rama. But King Dasaratha's wife, Rama's stepmother, wanted her own son, Prince Bharat, to be king. She knew that Dasaratha loved her so much that he would give her anything she desired. So she went to him and asked him to banish Rama to the forest of Dandak for fourteen years and make Bharat king. And although Dasaratha was both angry and upset, he did exactly as she asked.

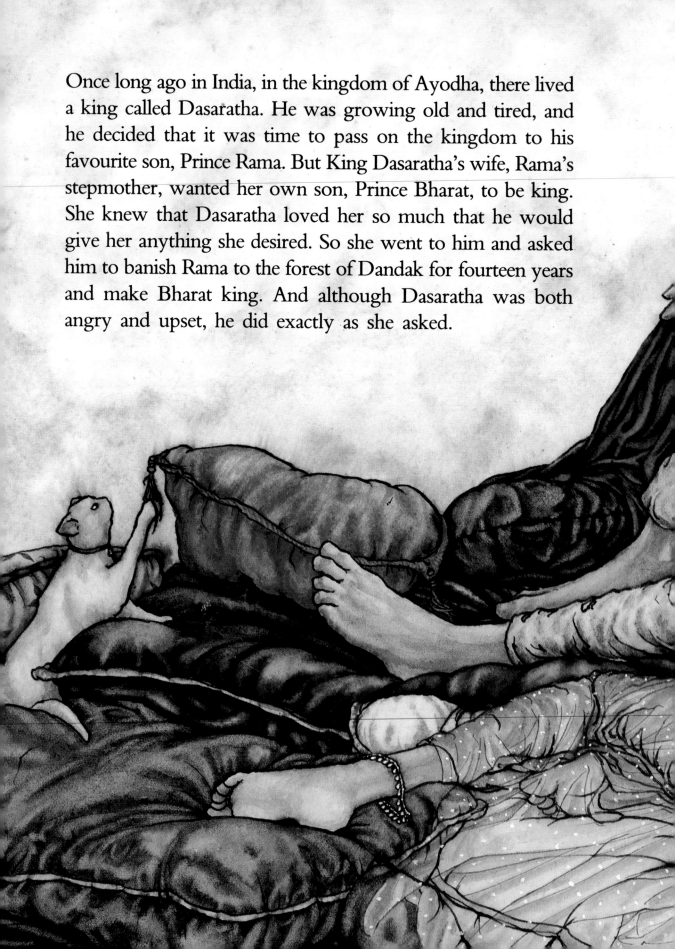

The next day, Rama left his father's palace with his wife, Sita, and his brother, Lakshman, and went into the dark forest of Dandak. On their journey they met an old wise priest who warned them that demons hid within the shadows of the trees. He gave Rama a quiver of magic arrows to protect himself from the evil in the forest and told the travellers to search for the Vale of Panchavati. 'There you will be safe,' he said.

After many days travelling, Rama, Sita and Lakshman came to the Vale of Panchavati. Remembering what the old man has said, they built themselves a house from hardened earth and bamboo. And so they lived happily for many years.

Then one day a little faun came running out of the forest. It was the most beautiful animal Sita had ever seen and she begged Rama to catch it for her. Leaving Lakshman to look after his wife, Rama chased the little faun deeper and deeper into the forest. It led him down winding paths, through tangles of branches, into darkened thickets, until he was completely lost — and yet no matter how fast he ran, he could never quite catch it.

Suddenly, Sita thought she heard Rama's voice crying from the forest: 'Help me, Lakshman, help me!'

Lakshman ran off into the forest to try to find his brother, leaving Sita feeling frightened and alone. No sooner was he out of sight than an ugly little old man appeared on the doorstep of the hut, as if from nowhere. But as Sita watched, the little old man grew, his face changed, his dirty clothes vanished and there stood Ravana, the king of the demons!

Sita screamed but there was no one to hear her — Rama and Lakshman were now both lost in the heart of the forest. Ravana had sent the little deer to draw Rama away from the house and then tricked Lakshman with false cries for help to make sure he would find Sita alone.

Now, with a wave of his hand, Ravana summoned his magic chariot and he swept Sita up and away into the sky, over the forest and across the plains and mountains beyond, until at last they crossed the sea and landed on the demon island of Lanka.

Rama and Lakshman wandered for many hours in the forest until they finally found their way home. As soon as they saw that Sita had gone, they realized that they had been tricked and that Sita had been taken away by the demons.

Picking up his quiver of magic arrows and his bow, Rama set out with Lakshman in search of his wife. But although they travelled for many miles through the forests and across the plains and mountains, they found no sign of her.

Then one day, as they were crossing a wooded mountain pass, an enormous ape jumped down from a rock onto the path in front of them. He bowed. 'I am Hanuman,' he said, 'the captain of the Vanar tribe of monkeys.' He told them how he had seen Ravana's chariot flying through the sky with Sita aboard, and he promised Rama that he and his army would help in the search for Sita. He clapped his paws together and suddenly, down from the rocks, came hundreds and hundreds of monkeys.

Rama and his new army travelled on across the mountains until they reached the highest peak, where a vulture sat stretching his wings in the sunlight. He, too, had seen Ravana and Sita; and he had seen the chariot land on the island of Lanka.

'You will never get her back now, Rama,' he croaked. 'For the sea between here and the island is stormy and dangerous and no one except the demons can cross it.'

But Rama would not give in and he led his army on and down to the seashore, where the angry waves grew higher and higher, beating wildly against the rocks. Rama could not see how he would ever reach the island and was about to despair when suddenly, out of thin air, a mighty demon prince appeared.

'I am Vibishan, Ravana's brother,' he cried. 'I hate my brother as much as you and so I have come to help you destroy him. But first we must build a bridge to the island from trees and rocks and anything else we can find.'

Immediately, all the monkeys went to work. They tore up whole tree trunks and broke off boulders from the cliffs, and hurled them into the sea.

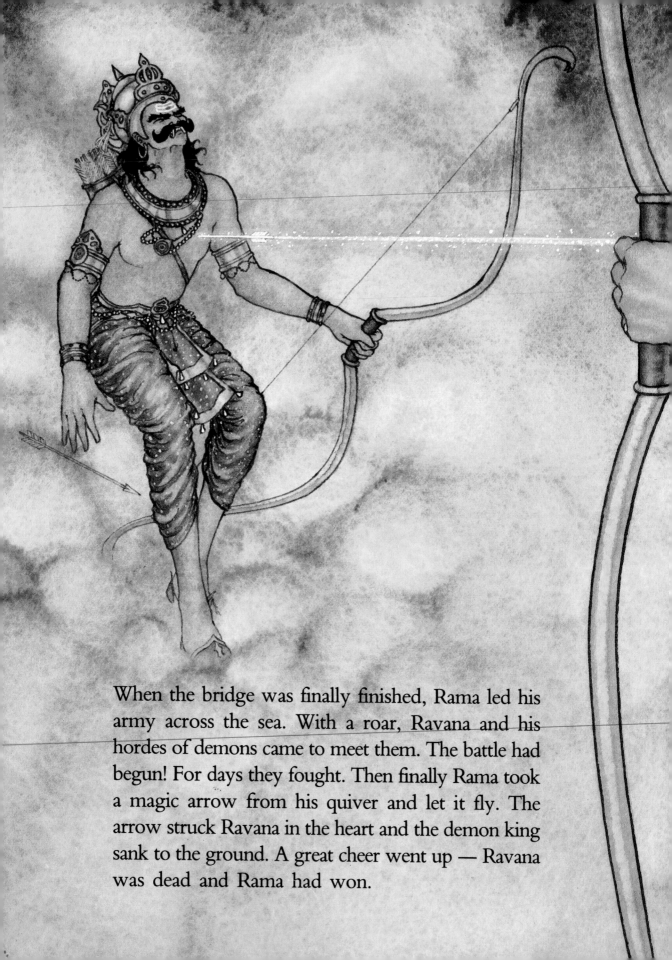

When the bridge was finally finished, Rama led his army across the sea. With a roar, Ravana and his hordes of demons came to meet them. The battle had begun! For days they fought. Then finally Rama took a magic arrow from his quiver and let it fly. The arrow struck Ravana in the heart and the demon king sank to the ground. A great cheer went up — Ravana was dead and Rama had won.

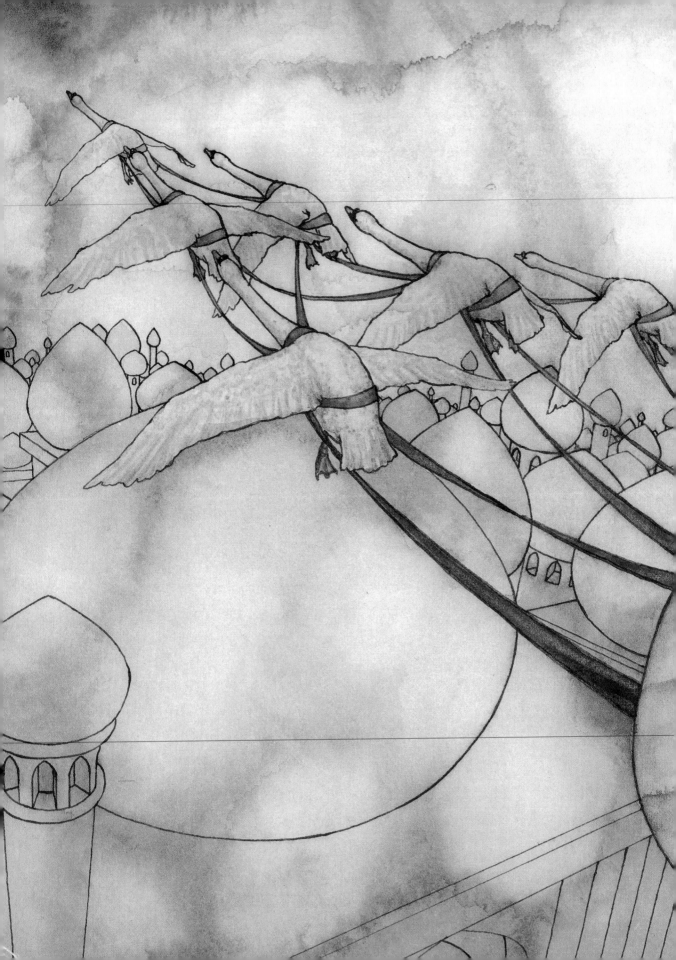

Rama and Sita were together again at last and the streets of Lanka were filled with the sounds of laughter and singing as the celebrations began. Fourteen years had passed since Rama had first left his father's palace and his exile had now ended. It was time for him to return to Ayodha. Vibishan gave him a magic chariot drawn by swans and, as everyone cheered from below, Rama and Sita flew up into the clouds to begin their last journey home.